The Stepmother

EMMANUEL UCHE

This edition first published in paperback by
Michael Terence Publishing in 2023
www.mtp.agency

ISBN 9781800945852

Michael Terence
Publishing

This book is dedicated to all stepchildren and their like who go through hard times in their various homes.

My special thanks go to my family and Alana Fajobi for their contribution and support in making the dream come true.

Above all, I give God the glory.

Contents

1: A Broken Relationship 1

2: Edwin Marries Victoria 12

3: Attitudes of Some Stepmothers 22

4: The Unreliable Friends.. 31

5: The Visit of James' Mother.................................. 39

6: James the Man With a Large Heart 52

7: The Power of Forgiveness 60

1

A Broken Relationship

The power of nature over humanity in the area of procreation and other issues cannot be questioned. Most times we are brought into situations and conditions we do not have control over because we never bargained for them. But we marry to fulfil the purpose of nature over humanity to procreate. Often, we have a separation between husband and wife in a marriage due to one reason or the other. Sometimes, this separation occurs after one or more children have been born to the couple.

After the breakup or the dissolution of the marriage, the children are left under the care and custody of their father according to the law of the land. Then when the man marries another wife to build his home and continue his life, the new wife automatically becomes the stepmother of his children from his past marriage or relationship. She comes in and assumes the responsibility for the welfare of the children she has inherited in the marriage. Sometimes the experience of the children in the hands of the stepmother is more than the eyes can see or imagine.

Edwin had a relationship with Anne but unfortunately, they separated after the birth of their child, James. Edwin's parents insisted on the separation because they saw the incompatibility between Edwin and Anne based on tribe. Secondly, their traditions and customs did not permit the firstborn in the family to marry outside his tribe.

A sharp disagreement and argument ensued between Edwin and his parents. "I love Anne, she is a good girl from a good background," Edwin responded in his defence of his parents' argument.

"We know you love her, but we cannot go contrary to our customs and traditions," said his parents.

Now, it was a case of tradition against true love and being reasonable.

Anyway, it was a tough moment for Edwin as every effort he made to win his parents over to accept Anne as their daughter-in-law failed. He also imagined how difficult it would be for him to break the news of his parents' position to her and live his life without Anne. Unfortunately, the happy and promising marriage envisaged by both Anne and Edwin would soon be sacrificed, slaughtered on the altar of tribe, using customs and traditions as an excuse. When Edwin realised he could not change his parents' stance, he shortened his stay and left in anger.

As soon as he got back to the city, he invited his friend and a cousin for a chat at a pub that was a few streets away from his house. Gilbert and Jonah honoured the invitation. Gilbert his friend, arrived first and waited for Edwin and Jonah. While he was waiting, the waiter approached him to take his order. Edwin and Jonah arrived almost at the same time before the waiter came back with Gilbert's order. As he was about to leave, Edwin and Jonah placed an order of what they wanted, and Edwin paid for all.

After the exchange of greetings and request for information on home news from both Gilbert and Jonah, Edwin went straight to the reason he invited them.

"I've had issues with my parents after I told them about Anne and my son."

Jonah was quick to ask, "What kind of issues and what do you mean?"

"My parents refused my proposal to marry Anne because she is not from the same tribe as me," Edwin replied with pain in his voice that almost betrayed his emotions.

"This is serious in this modern age," chorused both Gilbert and Jonah. "But what do you intend to do next?"

"I want to ignore them and that was why I invited both of you here; to solicit your support."

"Ok, we have your back, count on us and go ahead," they said to him.

Edwin was delighted and impressed by their proposed support. As they began to discuss other matters as a family, Jonah ordered more drinks to celebrate the arrival of Edwin's son. They really had a good time at the bar as they emptied their bottles and followed Edwin home for more talks on the issues of life as well as to see Anne and the baby.

Anne was excited but curious to see them as Edwin had gone out immediately after visiting his parents.

Upon their arrival, Anne asked, "Is everything alright?"

"Yes," Edwin replied. "They followed me home to see you and the baby."

Anne went back to the kitchen to prepare dinner while Edwin and the visitors discussed politics, football and religion. But before Anne could finish, both Gilbert and Jonah left for their homes.

She served dinner and after they had eaten and Edwin had complimented her on the good meal, she asked him about his parents and their reaction to hearing the news of the arrival of their grandchild.

"Oh, they were in good health and delighted to hear about the arrival of their grandchild and they looked forward to seeing both of you soon," Edwin lied to cover up for his parents at that moment. Anne was excited, looking forward to the day Edwin would take them to see his parents.

As they lay in bed, with James their son in the middle, they were filled with joy and happiness and began to make plans for their future as husband and wife together. But inwardly, Edwin was worried about his parents' reaction to his decision to marry Anne. Though he did not betray his worry as they talked,

Anne being an intelligent girl, began to suspect and question his reactions during their discussion. She noticed that he was not free in some of his responses and she asked,

"Darling is anything the matter? I noticed you looked distracted as I was talking to you."

"Oh, nothing to worry about, I was carried away by something else."

"And what was that?" she asked.

"I said, do not worry about that, my love."

That was the end of the discussion before she fell asleep.

Really Edwin was troubled, yet he was determined to go ahead with his decision to marry Anne. Within him, he felt he had found true love in Anne, and both were happy with each other. He believed that a happy wife and a happy husband in a marriage will always make a happy life and home. He realised that their love for each other was as deep as the ocean and their respect for one another was immeasurable and great. As a result, he did not want anything to come between them, not even his parents. Unfortunately, this was far from his parents' conviction, position and perception. Edwin gradually saw Anne slipping away from him.

Sometimes in life, it is important to follow our minds, but it does not mean we should not seek advice on sensitive and important issues as they come our way, from people we trust and believe in. And when advice is given, it behoves us to sit back and weigh the pros and the cons of the advice before we begin to implement or reject it.

Soon after, Gilbert and Jonah discussed in detail the agenda of their meeting with Edwin. Gilbert asked Jonah for his opinion on the issue, and without wasting time, Jonah said unequivocally, "I will not support their marriage, I am on the same page as his parents."

Gilbert was surprised. "But he is your cousin, and he is counting on us to support him."

"I do not care, but he should not marry before us," Jonah said without mincing words.

"I see your point, and I think you are right," agreed Gilbert.

From that moment on, they resolved to work against Edwin. They felt that Edwin was making progress earlier in life than them. They failed to realise that there is no competition in destiny. Everyone has his or her own moment in life. Therefore, anyone in the position of Gilbert and Jonah to envy someone at the time of his or her success or breakthrough in life should know that he or she cannot change God's plan or purpose for that person. Unfortunately, they failed to know this as they resolved to work against Edwin. By doing this, they betrayed the bond of friendship and trust Edwin held with them.

Based on this resolution, both travelled to the village without the knowledge of Edwin. In the village, before

Edwin's parents, they presented a report of hatred and lies against Anne to discredit her and win the sympathy of Edwin's parents. They convinced them to stick to their resolution against Edwin marrying Anne.

This is the betrayal by Gilbert and Jonah of Edwin.

Good friends are meant to stand by each other in times of need and crises in their lives, but Gilbert and Jonah threw caution to the winds and allowed their selfish interests to cloud their sense of reason, to betray their townsman. Their actions were shrouded in lies, envy and hatred. Just remember, not all who laugh and play with us are our real and true friends. Remember Judas's kiss.

Unluckily, Edwin's parents did not read between the lines to see the hatred and envy against their son from his so-called friend and cousin. But many parents today are like Edwin's parents, as unstable as the stream to believe stories said against their child or children by their friends without verification.

They believed what they heard about Anne and used this as the reason to prevent Edwin from marrying her. It is painful when people we trust and believe in, trust and believe an outsider's report more than our own. When relationships are broken by parents, they do not know the pain, agony and heartbreak the principal actors and actresses go through. Edwin's parents did not know what these two love birds would go through for their love.

Broken relationships lead to the emergence of a stepmother where a child or children are involved. The final decision of Edwin's parents to stop the relationship was their greatest undoing or mistake. Edwin's parents failed to understand that the report from Gilbert and Jonah was due to their being jealous that Edwin would marry before them. Gilbert and Jonah reminded themselves how Edwin bought a car before them, lived in a two-bedroom apartment, living large, while they were still living in a one-bedroom apartment. Their jealousy began the moment they saw Anne as a gorgeous, well-mannered and successful lady with exotic charms and class that could stop traffic.

One day, Edwin visited to inform Gilbert and Jonah of his plans to take Anne and his son to the village for his parents to see them. He did not know that they had just come back from the village too. So, on a scheduled date, Edwin and Anne travelled to his village to see his parents. They were well received on arrival and immediately, Edwin's mother saw the traits and qualities of a good wife in Anne, but she could not go against their plans and resolutions. After dinner, they broke the news of their decision to both Edwin and Anne, Anne broke down in tears and Edwin held her to console her, but he could not hold back his tears as both wept on each other's shoulders. They were feeling bad and seeing the emerging end of a promising future marriage. Parents should consider the pain and trauma their wards would go through before wading into relationships of their children to act like Edwin's parents.

Sometimes, the price we pay for trusting friends and relations on sensitive issues that concern or are important to us can be frustrating. Edwin paid the price when Gilbert and Jonah became instruments to his parents' position against his proposition.

Edwin and Anne came back to the city almost immediately. It was a tough moment for both as they resolved to go ahead with their plans to be together as husband and wife. Their love for each other was as solid as a rock and as deep as the ocean and so no amount of sand filling in form of opposition could fill the ocean of their love for each other to stop them.

Unfortunately, when parents are involved in decision-making for their child, especially in their love life, it becomes a problem for that child. And any form of disobedience may attract negative words against that child from his or her parents.

Edwin realised this and felt it would not be easy for him to go against his parents' wish, but how he would pass his feelings and fears to Anne was his greatest worry. When the pressure became too much for him to bear, he reluctantly called Anne and said,

"As much as I love you and had vowed nothing would separate us, I find it hard to go against my parents' wishes because of the consequences in future."

Anne was thrown off balance and she did not know when she released a fart and said, "That means, you do not love me if you would allow your parents to decide your future for you."

Edwin tried to defend himself, but the words could not connect as he was confused and worried too. Eventually, he said,

"Darling, please forgive and bear with me for not being able to defend our love at this point before my parents."

Anne could not believe everything happening, but because she was a woman of strong will, and had strength of character, she controlled herself and waited for the day she would move out of Edwin's house.

Always remember that in every life situation, people are forced to take decisions when they are pushed against the wall. Sometimes they live to regret that decision later in life; sometimes it pays off well. It was not long before both Edwin and his parents realised their mistakes and began to regret their actions when it was discovered that the reports of Gilbert and Jonah against Anne were in fact, lies. Then it dawned on them that their hasty decision was a total miscalculation of judgement, like a broken egg that cannot be gathered again.

After this, both Anne and Edwin moved on with their lives and got married respectively to their newfound loves. Unfortunately, neither of them had a blissful and happy marriage; they did not enjoy their newfound love. They endured their marriages and Edwin wished he could change the tide.

Life becomes frustrating and painful when relations and friends push us away from our happiness all in the name of trying to protect us. Edwin's parents regretted their actions while Edwin paid the price.

Yes, most parents regret their actions against their children when the truth is eventually known. But what gave some of these parents the guts to make decisions for their children? Some of them feel that their child does not have the capacity to make good decisions for himself or herself. They would always defend their actions by saying, "What a child sees standing, an adult sees sitting down." Based on this, they assume they have the capacity to make decisions and rule over their children. Parents should allow their children to make certain decisions about their future, especially when it comes to marriage. Life is better and sweeter when you marry the person you love and vice versa.

Gilbert and Jonah celebrated the success of their treachery against Edwin. Though they maintained their relationship with him, he did not know their role in his woes.

It is quite frustrating when our close friends and relations are fingered as the source of our problems. Be careful. Parents should listen more to their children on issues that trouble them and give them sleepless nights, rather than following the crowd of liars against them.

2

Edwin Marries Victoria

After the dissolution of Edwin's relationship with Anne by his parents, they found a more fitting woman for him to marry from a nearby village. It is good to obey our parents, but sometimes they are not always right in deciding for us. Although they are required to be around to guide us, they are not meant to decide for us.

Edwin got married to Victoria with all the fanfare their customs and traditions allowed. Yes, we marry for love, and it is expected that the love we profess for marrying each other should also be extended to children from the past relationship of either the man or the woman. At this point, they become the stepmother or stepfather to the child. This was the case with James when Madam Victoria became his stepmother.

Love drives a man to travel miles and sometimes he climbs hills and mountains to marry the woman of his choice. He also sacrifices his rights and privileges and plays the fool even in the face of provocations and insults. He plays the fool to get what he wants because if a situation in life becomes a win-win issue then both of us are losers. On this premise, we play the fool to get what we want. This is also applicable to the woman who gives up her father's name to bear the husband's name, all in the name of love and marriage. But it becomes painful and heartbreaking when parents come in to decide for their child on the grounds that the child lacks the capacity to know what is good for them. More so, when either of the couple fails to live up to their vows to the other.

Now as a stepmother, Victoria pretended to love and care for James, but it was only to be for that moment. When God blessed her with her own child, then the true picture of her character began to manifest. Maltreatment began, but she failed to realise that this stepchild she maltreated could be the shining star of the family. Because she had come into the marriage with the attitude and mentality of killing the stepchild before he grew up, she acted unreasonably and intensified her wicked and barbaric acts. This mindset is common in some stepmothers.

It becomes painful when situations like this happen in a home. Some stepmothers would not show their resentment and hatred to the stepchild immediately, until they have their own child, the same way Victoria behaved. From that moment on, they will begin to unleash their venom of wickedness on the innocent stepchild. Offences their children would commit and get a verbal reprimand for, get a serious warning or even beating when the stepchild commits that. Some stepmothers make life unbearable for the stepchild. They make sure the stepchild no longer enjoys the liberties others enjoy at home. They make the stepchild a stranger and a slave in the house. This is absurd, painful and unacceptable, but we cannot help it when the man of the house is either unaware or complicit with the wife. Sometimes he believes more in whatever is said and pays less attention to the child. Fathers who do not have time to listen to their children before they act are not doing right and will one day live to regret their actions. Sometimes they act this way because they believe the stepmother can never be wrong.

While some stepmothers show half-hearted love and affection shredded in hypocrisy and wickedness to the stepchild, some fathers do not know this, because some of the stepmothers are crafty and clever, even powerful in that they control the home. This makes it difficult for their husband to correct and reprimand them. And whenever he does correct her, it would make no difference to what the stepchild is going through already. But the reality that the child's troubles have just begun as far as the stepmother is concerned makes it more painful as the father is not always at home to witness or protect them. This was the case for James when on one occasion Edwin suspected ill-treatment and acted against it.

Some stepmothers are so strong to the point that when the man of the house tries to stamp his authority in the home, to stop or check their excesses against the stepchild, they would ask him to choose between them and the child. Here, the man is in a tight situation and if he is not wise and falls into the trap of making a choice, the stepchild's woes are aggravated. On the other hand, some fathers would stand for the truth to defend and protect the child, they make sure their wife does not pour her frustration on the stepchild. Others will flow with the tide in the house and the stepchild suffers.

Some stepmothers would do all within their powers to kill the destiny of the stepchild, especially when they discover the stepchild is more endowed and their destiny is brighter than their own children. This is what happens when parents wade in and break marriages or when divorce occurs in a marriage and another woman comes in as a stepmother. The children from that relationship are at the mercy of whoever comes in as a stepparent.

Now Victoria had moved into her matrimonial home as wife and as the stepmother to James, legally married to Edwin according to custom and tradition. Both husband and wife enjoyed their early times together until the moment Edwin was granted custody of James. From that moment, there was a clash of emotions between Victoria and Edwin. Her hatred for James was not hidden and every effort made by Edwin to pacify her and make her treat James as her son was like a tall order meant for the kangaroos.

James was just five years old when he came to live with his father. Upon his arrival, Victoria was in control of the house, and she restricted him from enjoying certain privileges, especially when Edwin was not at home. Before James' arrival at the house, Victoria had given birth to two boys. We can now see where her attitude and actions towards James stemmed from.

One day, the situation in the house was made known to Edwin when he observed that everybody in the house was in the sitting room watching a programme on their black and white television set, but James was in the children's room alone. In his worry and curiosity, he called James to the parlour and asked,

"James, what were you doing alone in the room while everyone was in the sitting room?""

"Big mummy asked me not to sit and watch television with them," James told his father. Edwin was pained, but he controlled his anger and ordered him to sit down immediately.

Edwin waited until the children slept before he began to talk to his wife about what James had said. Many a time, the way we react to issues reported to us by someone close and dear can aggravate the situation, and this could be detrimental to the cause of the situation and the person we intended to protect and fight for. So, Edwin was careful and chose his words wisely.

The matter was resolved immediately because of the way Edwin handled it, and Victoria had no reasons for her actions. But that was the tip of the iceberg as the myriad of dos and don'ts that James had to obey remained unnoticed and unattended to. Living with some stepmothers is like living in hell, as some of their acts are covered with pretences of love in the open and they act like the devil incarnate in secret.

One fateful day, James could not finish his house chores before lunch, and when he saw his half-brothers eating, he went and carried his plate of food too. It was not long afterwards that Madam Victoria came into the house and saw him with his plate of food, and she queried, "Have you finished your house chores, you son of a viper?"

"No, Ma," James replied.

Name-calling by the stepmother to the stepchild was not new and so it did not trouble James. In her usual manner, Victoria collected the plate of food from him after a pull on his ear and proceeded to empty the food into the dustbin and said, "Finish your house chores and remember no food again for you till tonight." James was surprised to see his stepmother do that to his plate of food.

James was confused, and the fear of the unknown spread helplessness all over him as he did not know what to do at that moment, especially in his hungry condition. He could not explain the reasons behind her actions. But this was just the tip of the iceberg compared to some of the experiences other stepchildren go through at the hands of their stepmothers.

Regrettably, some stepmothers have sold themselves into wickedness and evil that they do not even remember to think of death. Well, the reason we live and do things the way they suit us is that we do not remember that one day we will die and probably leave our children to another stepmother to care for them. But honestly, if we remember this and recognise the fact that there is also a payday for our actions on earth, then we should act with love and caution in our dealings with one another, and this will make the world we live in a better place for all of us.

When Edwin could not bear the hatred of Victoria against James, he invited his parents over for their intervention. According to him, they were responsible for their marriage and of course, she was their choice for him. Upon their arrival, Madam Victoria received them with open arms and began to treat James like a human being. She showed love to James to cover up, though it was a plastic and cosmetic love.

One day, unknown to her that one of them was watching her, she betrayed her hatred and dislike of James in her attitude towards him. A leopard cannot hide his colours. To broker peace, they called for a meeting with both Edwin and Victoria. In that meeting, Edwin's father said to Victoria.

"We were responsible and instrumental to your marriage to our son, so do not act in a way to let us down to break the family ties between your family and ours. We observed your attitude towards James, and we were not pleased with what we saw. Let it be the last."

"I hear sir, and I promise to change towards him and take him as my son too," she assured them.

They were pleased to hear her response and they left after some days. This is one of the mistakes parents make when they enter a marital alliance on behalf of their children with another family. What this type of marriage alliance does is that sometimes it brings two incompatible people together as husband and wife.

To be fair to Victoria, she changed towards James and relaxed some of the secret laws he had to obey. She kept her promise and Edwin was pleased too. But it was not long before she devised other means to deal with James. Victoria was mean and barely educated. Edwin's parents reviewed all they saw when they got back to the village and began to regret their refusal to allow Edwin to marry Anne. They saw the wickedness in Victoria and realised she hid her true character from the onset to enable them to approve of her marriage with their son.

Even her own parents saw her as a wicked girl in her growing up, but because of the agreement both families had entered after her birth and the fact that she was their daughter, they could not stop the marriage; if they had, it might break the bond of friendship between both families. Parents, please do not mortgage the future and happiness of your children by entering into a marital agreement with another family on behalf of your children, just because you want to maintain your friendship.

Naturally, Victoria packaged herself as a good girl on her first visit to Edwin's parents. She covered some of her bad traits. This is quite typical of some people, so look before you leap into marriage or else you will be like a fish out of water panting for air to survive in the long run if you make the wrong choice. That was the kind of wife Edwin's parents found for him. It was too late for him to cry when he realised his mistake.

In homes where stepmothers exist, some of them are vicious and inconsiderate. The stepchild does not live his life, but his life lives him as he lives through fear and pain in his father's house. Most times these acts are done out of wickedness. And wickedness is unacceptable in our existence, so always remember your background and where you come from. Do not be the product of your environment. The fact you have a background of evil and wickedness does not mean you should be mean and vicious in life. We do not have to follow the crowd to do evil, rather we need to chart a new path to do good to people and shine like the brightest star.

James as a teenager was well-behaved and studious. He did not allow what was happening in the house to shape his life, so he was obedient to the core and was liked and admired by all in his environment.

One day he did not finish his house chores before he went to do his homework. Victoria was angry at him for abandoning his house chores for homework, and in her rage, she raised her hand to hit James. James got up and held her hand in the air. This act of boldness by James annoyed her more and she said to him,

"Oh, you are now grown to suspend my hand in the air. Anyway, let's watch and see, but lest you forget, if you think you will rule your father's house you are making a mistake. To be honest with you, and as far as I have life, you cannot rule over my children."

James answered her, 'My survival in this life and this house is in the hands of God because I believe in Live and let Live."

Wherever he got the courage to stop her from hitting him and saying those words to her was a big surprise to him. This was one of his experiences as a teenager in his father's house. And this is peculiar to other stepchildren in their various homes.

3

Attitudes of Some Stepmothers

Most stepchildren go through hard and terrible experiences in their father's house, and that leaves them with no option other than to put their faith in God. Some women have an amazing capacity for deceit and appear like angels outwardly to deceive the unsuspecting family they want to be married into. They hide their real characters, and when they are finally married into that family, they show love and care to everyone including the man's child or children from his previous relationship. But after a while, their true colours manifest showing the venom of a viper.

Some stepmothers will gradually stamp their authority on the home the moment they have their own child. Most times, this authority is to the detriment of the stepchild who is always at the receiving end of their wickedness. They begin to set out tasks as a daily routine for the stepchild, which they will do before their breakfast, lunch or even dinner. While their own children live like Lords, Kings and Queens in the same house. The stepchild invariably becomes the slave to the family. What an irony of fate against the stepchild.

James had a friend who lived with his stepmother in the same neighbourhood and his name was Gerald. Gerald's mother walked out of her marriage because her husband was cheating on her. But that was not the best decision to make as she did not put the welfare of Gerald and his brother Kenneth into consideration. Gerald's father went ahead and married his mistress. It was not the best decision for him to make, but he took that decision.

It was not long before Susan moved into the house and became a stepmother to Gerald and Kenneth. She was quite an exceptional stepmother with the milk of human kindness in her veins. She was natural and kind-hearted, with no deception in her actions towards everyone in the house. She was just herself and as innocent as an angel. The way she treated Gerald and Kenneth, made them not feel the absence of their mother. Susan was quite an amazing woman. Her behaviour and attitude in the house showed that she was not the kind of stepmother that sees stepchildren as a product of an accident in a family. She did not do anything within her powers to annihilate, maltreat, intimidate or frustrate Gerald and his brother. She detached herself from the mentality of the reality that Gerald and his brother were not her biological children hence she treated them well. This should be a lesson to other stepmothers.

While James was lamenting and bemoaning the ill-treatment his stepmother carried out towards him, Gerald and his brother were of a different view and opinion about stepmothers. Different strokes for different people. This obviously tells us that some stepmothers can be loving and caring too.

One fateful day, as James was performing his daily forced chores, he remembered a song and began to sing.

"For work, they remembered the stepchild, but for reward and recognition, they side-lined him, my mother, why did you leave and abandon me to the care of another woman?""

What a pathetic and heart-rending rendition by James. Though, it was not his mother's fault, it was a clear case of custom, tradition and belief fighting against the reality of true love between two love birds.

Ideally, leaving your marriage for whatever reason and allowing another woman to come in as a stepmother to your children is senseless on the part of the person involved. Using James as our case study, this decision will expose the child to hatred, maltreatment and mental torture from the actions of the stepmother. It brings sorrow and pain to the child. It makes it difficult for the child to live their life to the fullest or reach their potential. So, no matter the provocation and quarrel in the house, provided it is not a life-threatening situation, do not abandon your child and home to the care of another woman. It is quite unacceptable. And parents should be careful and cautious not to interfere in their ward's relationships.

Whatever the situation, we should always remember there is no perfect marriage or relationship. Rather we build both with our hands through good character and tolerance to bring about perfection in the end. If mothers who abandoned their children to the care of a stepmother knew what they went through in their absence, they would rethink before they left their marriage. Anne's case was not a case of abandoning her home, but a clear case of tradition against true and sincere love.

Edwin got on with his work, while James was left in the care of his stepmother. He did not know what happened to James in his absence. James pretended that all was well at home. He did not complain about anything for fear of the consequences. He became taciturn.

It is quite ridiculous and unacceptable for children to pretend that all is well at home when they are abused for fear of what would happen if they complained. Most mistreated stepchildren die in silence, and some go as far as committing suicide when they can no longer stand the mental torture. Ironically, some careless and carefree parents do not know this, and when they know, they do not take the complaints seriously. Parents, please spend time with your children, especially when there is a stepmother or father to your child. No matter your busy schedule, spend some moments with the child as they may be going through hell in your absence.

Abuse of the stepchild is not peculiar to stepmothers alone. Some stepfathers are culprits too. Some of them abuse the stepchild sexually if she is a female. It is quite unreasonable and nauseating. Generally, the abuse is more pronounced with stepmothers. But whatever happens, let us know that we are one, filled with water and blood flowing in our veins as created by God. The only difference between the stepmother, the stepfather and the stepchild is our conscience, and it remains an open wound which only truth, love, tolerance and understanding for one another can heal. Therefore, stepmothers and stepfathers should distance themselves from the conspiracy to kill or harm the stepchild.

Edwin's situation was quite pathetic. It is inappropriate for parents to force their children to marry against their will. No matter the bond of agreement between a family and another. It is not enough reason to force your child to marry from that family, thus mortgaging their happiness, even when they are not compatible. Children should be allowed to marry their choice when they are ready to marry.

The picture of wickedness some stepmothers portray in the home against the stepchild often paints an air of fear in the lives of the stepchild who sees him or herself as a stranger in the home. Not only that, but some stepmothers take control of the home by also turning the hearts and minds of their husbands against the stepchild. They achieve this through lies against the stepchild. At this point, the stepchild is in trouble because their source of defence and protection in the home is now against them. And the aim of all these is to secure the future of their biological children at the expense of the stepchild.

Some stepmothers decorate the bodies of their stepchildren with a rainbow of bruises in their bid to stamp their authority on the stepchild. Sometimes, this brazen act of wickedness has led to the untimely death of stepchildren. But James in all these circumstances remained resolute and did not allow himself to be distracted because he believed that every situation in his life was like a storm, that would pass away before the victory at the end of it.

Some stepmothers are like the weevil in the bean seed that eats up the bean to leave the empty shell and whenever the bean seed is pressed between your fingers, it turns to dust. This is the same way the life of the stepchild is gradually destroyed. Fathers should be careful how they react to complaints from their wives against their stepchildren.

These acts no doubt affect the stepchild negatively. It creates a scenario of not feeling wanted in the home in the psyche of the stepchild. Sometimes, the stepchild losses their joy and confidence the moment they get close to the house after playing and smiling with friends. The smile vanishes the moment they remember what awaits them at home. The fear of the unknown sets in.

This mindset prevents the stepchild from rising to their potential in life. But that should not deter the stepchild because, with sheer determination and willpower, they will emerge victorious. You cannot keep a good man down forever. The only difference between failure and success is your determination to rise and move on to achieve your aim when your oppressors feel you are down forever. Rising against their expectations makes the difference. Try and rise and do not wait to be counted out. Legendary Mohammad Ali the greatest of all time in boxing, succinctly said,

"If my mind can conceive it. And my heart can believe it. Then I can achieve it."

This was the mindset of the greatest of all time in the boxing ring. So, whatever you aspire to in life, even in the face of hatred and wickedness from anyone around you, should be achieved. Go ahead and take the first step.

However, some stepmothers fail to realise that their actions invariably help to make the stepchild become strong to face the reality of the challenges of life. Sometimes, it turns out to be a preparatory ground for the success of the stepchild later in life if the child remains focused. Unknown to some of these stepmothers, their own children become failures in home management. Some of them do not even know how to light the stove, let alone cook what someone can eat. They do not know how to wash plates or even their clothes, because the stepchild does the house chores. But in future, the biological children of the stepmother become vulnerable, a liability and a nuisance to themselves.

A hard beginning makes a happy ending. So, do not give up as a stepchild in the face of your travails in your father's house, you are in training. Again, if mothers who abandoned their children to the care of another woman, knew the trauma and pain these children went through, they would have second thoughts before leaving their marriage.

Edwin for his part never had peace or happiness in his home. He sacrificed his sense of reasoning to the altar of fear by allowing people to decide his future. He failed to fight his battles to protect his love. Love is like a two-edged sword with happiness and pain on either side. He realised it late and now he felt like a fish out of the water panting for survival as he wished he could turn the hands of the clock of his life back, to bring Anne back to his life again.

But it is always too late to cry when the head is off. It was too late for Edwin now, as Anne had moved on too. He realised that the decision he made due to the pressure from his parents over Anne affected him negatively. In other words, we will always live with the decisions we make in life as the choices we make control our actions and our actions determine and control our life. So, always sit back and think before you make or take any decision. Never make decisions when you are under pressure. And never make decisions to please people on issues that will determine your future.

Edwin wanted to turn back time to bring Anne back after he saw the attitude of Victoria towards James, but he could not. He observed that Victoria had the mentality of 'kill the stepchild before he grows up', which is the mindset or attitude of some stepmothers in the home. But people who mistreat or maltreat other people's children, because they can do so, should remember that their own children are also vulnerable to similar treatments when they are away. Bearing this in mind, stepmothers should stop seeing their stepchildren as rivals to their own children, as that is the root cause of their hatred towards them. Rather we should see ourselves as partners in progress in our various families. It is a painful reality to imagine the psychological and emotional trauma some stepchildren go through at the hands of their stepparent. And this has made some of them make rash decisions. Let's show love to them.

The world we live in would be a better place if we treated everyone well and allowed our love for one another to flow effortlessly like the river, without opposition and hindrance, irrespective of gender, colour and status. Everyone has the right to live because we are all in transit here on Earth. Wickedness should not be part of our existence, especially where stepmothers are involved in a home. The attitude of some to put the stepchildren to shame and turn them into a laughing stock should stop.

But James was smart, and he took control of every situation in his life. He worked hard to make his mark on whatever he did. He did not allow the feeling that he was like prey entering the ugly world where predators like Madam Victoria were waiting to capture and devour him in his father's house to knock him out.

So, then as a stepchild, do not panic when you see your stepmother or father as a result of the ill-treatment you go through at their hands, instead think and plan how to succeed in life and surprise them.

4

The Unreliable Friends

It is good to know the type of people you associate with and take as your friends. True friends are those that share the same views as you, stand by you in times of crisis and would not betray you.

Gilbert and Jonah married their girlfriends who were not from their tribes. Their own parents were wiser and maintained an attitude of, "She was your choice, and the two of you would live together, so, you have our blessings." These were the words of both parents. There was no opposition and even Edwin did not know about it until after they had completed all the marriage rites to their in-laws. What a world we live in. We live in a world where some people take delight in seeing other people down, even their friends. So, beware.

They had good and happy marriages to the point that Edwin considered them lucky and did not envy them. Even though they were instrumental in his unhappiness and the cold war in his home.

In our efforts to succeed and survive, there is always an element of luck with the people around us, as nature has its own plans for us. But Edwin was unlucky to have the friends that betrayed him around him. Life is what we make of it, and everyone has their moment, so, know when your time to rise and shine comes. Grab it and do not allow people to dictate to you what to do in case you lose focus.

Gilbert married Jane while Jonah married Cynthia. Both came from across the Niger almost from the same place Anne came from. Their parents believed their reports about their girlfriends and were more understanding than Edwin's parents to allow their sons to marry them irrespective of their tribe. It was easy for them because no one stood in the way against them as they did to Edwin. True friends should stand by each other and not play the role of Judas Iscariot when they are needed most.

Unreliable and untrustworthy friends are not worth associating with. They are as unstable as a chair with one leg off. They meander like a snake and move restlessly like the ocean until they achieve their aim. Know who you make friends with.

God blessed their marriages with children and material things. They made sure their children enjoyed the best things in life and they had peace in their homes. Unfortunately, Edwin never enjoyed peace in his home, and neither did James enjoy the best things in life which his half-brothers and sister enjoyed. This was the irony of being a stepchild to a vicious and overbearing stepmother, who wanted all the good things of life for her children alone.

One day James visited Gerald, after completing his house chores. Gerald's stepmother was in the parlour watching a programme on their black and white television with Gerald and his brother sitting beside her. James greeted her before Gerald got up and went outside to play with him and the other children in the neighbourhood. Soon after, Gerald's stepmother called, "Gerald, where are you?"

"I am playing with my friends," Gerald replied.

"Ok, my darling, lunch is ready, and do not keep us waiting. Please ask James to come with you," instructed his stepmother.

"Ok, Ma, we will be there in a jiffy," Gerald answered.

James was surprised at the friendly chat between Gerald and his stepmother and wished his stepmother could be as nice as this to the point of addressing him as her darling. But it was all wishes as he knew it would never happen. This was the pain and agony the unreliable friends of his father created for him.

James joined them at the table and had a good meal in a happy atmosphere. Really it was not the meal alone that made him happy, but the peaceful atmosphere in which they ate. He remembered how his stepmother would shout and bark at him, or even send him on errands in the middle of having his meal. What a price an innocent child paid for the activities of his father's friend and cousin and his grandparents as well.

James resolved not to be bothered and did not intend to disrespect his stepmother, so he resolved to enjoy his meal. But he hoped to correct the ills in his father's house in future, by deciding to use the reality of his childhood experience to spur him into victory in life. James also observed that they ate at the same dining table and from the same bowl of food, where portions were dished into everyone's plate by Gerald's stepmother. They ate in silence as one of the rules in the house was, 'No talking while eating.' At the end of the meal, James said to her, "Thanks for the meal, I really enjoyed it."

"You are welcome, my darling," Gerald's stepmother said.

At this point, James packed all the plates for washing, but Gerald's stepmother stopped him. He wanted to replicate what he normally did in his father's house after everybody had finished eating.

As they stepped out to continue their play, James said to Gerald, "You and your brother are lucky to have such a nice and caring stepmother."

"Yes, we are, she treats us like her own children."

Gerald had a stepbrother and a stepsister, and both worked and played together. In fact, no one knew they were half-brothers and sister. James wished again that his stepmother could be like Gerald's stepmother where he could play with his half-brothers and sister without restrictions.

Anyway, it tells us that not all stepmothers are as vicious and bad as Madam Victoria; there are some kind-hearted ones too. Really, Madam Victoria packaged herself to appear as innocent as an angel by pretending to be what she was not just to get what she wanted. Our world today is so full of people with questionable character, like Madam Victoria and this gives birth to deception. The only way to escape is to be mindful of who your friends are and who you intend to have dealings with.

If family connections brought Mrs Victoria and the wives of Gilbert and Jonah together, we cannot say anything about their attitudes in their various homes because they did not have a stepchild to care for. Upon their visit to see Victoria, they saw James performing his chores while Victoria and her children were having a siesta. They showed love and care to him and even helped him before they left and went to knock at the door to announce their presence. Madam Victoria opened the door and welcomed them. In the middle of their discussion, James came into the house to pick something up, and Madam Victoria shouted at him to get out, not minding the presence of her visitors.

To their dismay, what they saw confirmed their suspicions and what they heard from Victoria's neighbours about her attitude and behaviour towards James was quite reprehensible. So, on their way home, Gilbert's wife asked, "Why was Victoria so mean to treat James in such a way that showed as if he was not born the same as her own biological children were born?"

"I cannot explain, it beats my imagination how she shouted at him even in our presence. Anyway, human nature in relationships and behaviour cannot be determined when it involves stepchild and stepmother," answered Jonah's wife.

"I wonder, too," said Gilbert's wife.

Regardless, there was nothing either of them could do to help James as they did not want to gossip with their husbands. They wished his mother could visit and talk to Edwin to see if James could be treated like a human being and not like a slave, or even like a stranger in his father's house. Neither of them could talk to Victoria, because the day Gilbert's wife tried to advise her, she got the insult of her life with the final warning, "Mind your business, you have no right to tell me how to run my home." From that moment on, Gilbert's wife backed out, swallowed her pride and remained reticent, while maintaining the relationship. Inwardly, they were not happy with the treatment Victoria meted out to James. And little did they know that their husbands' actions were the reason James went through all that.

Sometimes, the problems we create by betraying someone because of envy leave a lot of scars on the map of history in the lives of the person concerned. If Gilbert and Jonah had realised what James would go through at the hands of Victoria, maybe they would not have betrayed Edwin. What can we say or do when the reason for their actions was purely based on envy? They were happily married and none of their children went through what James went through in his father's house. This is the irony of life when friends turn to betray one another for selfish reasons.

Stepmothers that have vicious characters and wicked minds towards their stepchildren, should remember that this world is like a parade ground where at the shout of 'about turn', the last becomes the first and the first becomes the last. So, your biological children you over-pamper, protect and cherish at the expense of the stepchild may become loafers and non-achievers in life and will not be able to care for you when you are old. There is a wise saying that there is no competition with destiny. Destiny can be delayed but it cannot be denied, so no matter what the stepmother or stepfather does to frustrate the stepchild, they should know that what would be, would be.

Therefore, knowing this, stepmothers who have a reputation to do evil and wickedness should know they cannot stop God's plan for the stepchild, even when it is established that their pretended love for the stepchild can be as different as night and day, that is neither here nor there. So, stepmothers be careful. That stepchild would be what God has destined him or her to be.

The love you professed to your husband should also be extended to the stepchild and vice versa. We know that a woman leaves her father's house and family to live with the man she loves in the name of marriage, and if that love is true, real and natural then the man's child should be loved as well. The ill-treatment of stepmothers to them should cease. While parents, on the other hand, should desist from selecting wives or husbands for their children in the name of tribe and religion, especially when a child is already involved. The consequence of their intervention leaves more to be desired such is the case of James and his stepmother.

5
The Visit of James' Mother

The visit of any woman to her former home will always be done with a mixture of feelings of jealousy and hatred from both women involved. Anne was excited the day she learnt Edwin had been transferred to the same city where she and her family lived. According to her, it would be another opportunity to see her son for the second time after she got married. At this point, she decided to pay Edwin a visit with the aim of seeing James. So, with the consent and approval of her husband, she visited the address Edwin sent her by post. On arrival, she saw James in an unkempt condition in the backyard with heaps of clothes for him to wash.

As soon as James saw her and recognised her as his mother, he dropped the clothes he was washing and rushed to embrace her. Immediately, mother and child began to cry in each other's arms. At some point, James asked, "Mom, why did you leave me?"

She did not answer but asked if his father was at home. "Yes, he is," James answered.

She released her grip on James and took some time to have a 360-degree look at him, and at the end, she asked, "When did you last have a haircut? Your hair is due for a cut." James did not answer for two reasons; first, he did not remember and again he was too excited.

Then she turned around and saw the heap of clothes in the corner where James was sitting before her arrival and asked, "Who was washing these clothes?"

"Mom, they were meant for me to wash."

"Why?" Anne asked with tears rolling down her cheeks. James began to cry too. After a moment of expressing their emotions, she wiped her eyes and drew him close again and asked him to lead her to their apartment.

Old lovers cannot be tamed from showing their affection for each other, even in the face of danger or adversity. Edwin got up from his seat and hugged Anne passionately to the envy and condemnation of Victoria who was having a discussion with Edwin. They did not mind her presence and reaction as they held onto each other for a while to the joy of James who was standing with hands akimbo watching them. This was another moment for them to meet again after a long time.

They were so excited to see each other again after they had met in a shopping mall some years back before her husband was transferred to their new base. Coincidentally, Edwin moved for greener pastures to the city without knowing that one day they would be in the same city again. So, on that fateful day, Edwin took James Christmas shopping before they bumped into Anne. It was like a dream to James when his father introduced Anne to him as his mother. This visit brought joy and excitement to them as it was another opportunity to see each other again.

Anne went out of her way to spoil James with gifts that day. James would always remember that day. Then after the hug, he ushered her to a seat. Victoria did not show any sign of recognising her presence as she was filled with rage, even after Anne greeted her. She did not respond to the greeting. Anne did not mind as she was too excited to see Edwin and James again after a long time.

After a while, Anne brought out from her bag some things she bought for both James and his half-brothers and sister and said to James, "Share with your brothers and sister." But before Edwin could thank her, Victoria interjected and said, "Do not give any of those things to my children, they do not need them." Anne was surprised at her outburst but decided to hold her peace. When Victoria observed neither Edwin nor Anne paid any more attention to her, she became restless and uncomfortable then she got up, hissed and walked out of the room.

Anne asked Edwin, "Why did Victoria react that way? Is this how you people live in this house?"

"Don't mind her, sometimes she acts like this. It appears she was in a bad mood," Edwin answered.

But the truth is that the hidden character of the wicked will always manifest when you least expect it. Victoria was evil and wicked; all she did was package herself as a good and caring woman on her arrival at

Edwin's house. She forgot that people who lied to gain favour will one day lose the favour through lies and bad behaviour. She pretended to be nice and caring, but the reality of her behaviour could not be hidden.

Anne went ahead to ask about their welfare and about Gilbert and Jonah.

"Everybody is fine, Gilbert and Jonah are doing great, and they are married with children."

"Oh, that is good to hear," Anne said. Then she asked, "But why was James looking so unkempt under your watch? And what was the meaning of what I saw him doing at the back of the house? I hope nobody has turned my son into a slave in this house?"

Edwin mumbled some words but could not give any satisfactory answer to Anne as he was as unstable as the ocean with his answers.

Listening to him with his explanations was like watching the grass grow. Anne imagined in her mind that Edwin had become like a tamed eagle with broken claws and a weak beak, so much so that he could not control the behaviour of his wife against James. And Anne's questions came even after Edwin had warned Victoria about James. She was displeased but what could she do when the man of the house was reluctant to act? They began to talk about other things and James was asked to go and have his bath before coming back to try on his new clothes, shoes and slippers. James and his siblings had a pair of slippers in the past but after they had worn out, Victoria replaced all except James' own. This meant James had to walk barefoot in the neighbourhood without his father noticing. Fathers should always watch over the welfare of their children especially when there is a stepchild and a stepmother in the home. James remained sober until this day when his mother visited and brought joy and laughter to him again through those gifts.

He had his bath and came back looking good in everything his mother had bought for him. He did not go back to wash those clothes, nor did anyone ask him to. But Victoria was filled with rage when she discovered that he did not go back to wash them. Anyway, she washed them after separating James' clothes from the rest. Ironically, James did not mind as that day was his happiest in that house. He never wanted his mother to go back. After some words of satisfaction from his mother when she saw the fitting of the clothes on him, James left them and went to play with his mates who were happy for him too on the visit of his mother.

Anne spent a long time talking with Edwin before she realised it was already late. They did not realise how long they had been talking. Anyway, whenever two love birds come together, the hours spent are never recognised. At the point of arranging her things to leave, Anne made a request to allow James to visit her, to enable him to see his other half-brothers and sisters. Edwin granted her request and James was delighted when he learnt about it.

On an agreed date, James' uncle came and drove him to his mother's house in another part of the city. Upon arrival, he received a warm reception and was celebrated by his mother, stepfather and his siblings. He felt at home for the first time in his life. They had lunch together just the same way he witnessed at Gerald's house. He was treated like a king and in the evening, his stepfather took him out for a walk and introduced him to his friends as his son. They came back with some gifts from some of his friends for James. James was excited and glad to be shown love by a man who was not his biological father.

By the time they came back, dinner was ready. He found out that his younger siblings were having their baths in turns, so he waited for his turn as the bathroom was not big enough to take more than two people at the same time. It was a rule in the house that you must bathe before dinner.

At the end of the exercise, dinner was served, and everyone ate in a quiet and conducive atmosphere. James wished he could replicate this in his father's house. But it was a tall order. After that, some of them engaged in one thing or the other while some watched the television, but James decided to be with his mother on the balcony of their house.

On the balcony, Anne asked James, "Tell me how you live with them and how they treat you?"

This was the opportunity he was waiting for to expose his experience in his father's house. James began to narrate how dirty plates in the house were meant for him to wash daily along with all the dirty clothes too. Sweeping the house was also part of his chores before breakfast. "In fact, they've turned me into a slave in that house."

His mother interjected by asking, "What happened to the clothes I saw you washing on the day I visited, did you continue to wash them after I left?"

"No, Ma, my father said I should not wash them, but my stepmother took mine out and washed the rest."

"No worries, but what happened then?" Anne asked.

"I have not washed their clothes since. I only wash mine and my father's."

Anne was delighted to hear this as James went ahead with other stories.

"Every house chore was left for me to perform without which I would not be given any food."

His mother was displeased as she shook her head in resentment and said to him, "Do not worry my son, you were undergoing training. So, do not despair, ok?"

His mother's words made him realise that the reality of his situation would only encourage him to move on and not allow the attitude of his stepmother towards him to bring him down. It was a form of training for him too as his mother said.

James really had a good time with his mother and siblings. Two days before his departure, his stepfather took him shopping. He had the choice of selecting whatever he wanted from the shelves. At the end of the shopping, James could not hide his joy when he told his stepfather that he did not want to go back to his father's house. But his stepfather encouraged him to go back and assured him that he could always visit them.

On the agreed date, his uncle came around and picked him up. James cried as he waved goodbye to them. His mother and siblings could not hold back their tears either. It was a moment to remember for James as he wished the love and kindness, he enjoyed here could be replicated in his father's house. But that was unlikely as the lioness in the home wished he never came back to the house. The cruelty of Madam Victoria and other stepmothers to their stepchild could be frustrating when the reasons behind such cannot be fathomed.

Back in his father's house, he was given a cold reception, which was not a surprise to him as he already expected it. His father had gone to work and only his stepmother and her children were at home. His half-brothers and sister could not jump to welcome him because their mother would scold and beat them. What a way to sow seeds of hatred and division in a home. James did not mind as he greeted his stepmother and went into the room to leave his bag. And after resting, he began to unpack his bag.

His half-brothers and sister would always play with him whenever their mother was not at home. But on this day, they could not contain their emotions, so when their mother came back from the market, she saw them still playing with James in the compound and shouted at them. She was furious and quickly pulled them away by the collars of their dresses, without a word until they got to their room. Then she said to them. "I have warned you all not to play with James." She demonstrated this with a pull on their ears.

Only Jane, the youngest had the guts to ask, "Why, Mummy? Is he not our brother?"

"No, he is not your brother." She turned to Hillary and Jackson and said, "These are your brothers."

Jane did not understand and to show her resentment and anger, she refused to have lunch and dinner that day. Imagine how Madam Victoria and even some stepmothers like her will pollute the minds of their children by sowing seeds of hatred and separation in a home.

When Edwin came back from work, he observed his little angel was not as happy and lively as she used to be as the baby of the house. He said to her, "Jane, you look so unhappy. What could be the reason behind that?"

She refused to talk to her father until he began to tease her and call her some pet names that always made her laugh and smile. She said, "Mummy pulled us by the collars of our dresses today when she came back from the market and saw us playing with James. She warned us not to play with him again and said that he is not our brother."

He was saddened to hear that and asked her if that was all that made her unhappy.

"Yes, Daddy, I know you told all of us that James is our elder brother, and we should play and respect him as well."

Edwin said to her, "Yes, I did, but do not mind your mother I will talk to her. Are you happy now?"

"Yes, Daddy."

"Then go and eat your food."

So, with joy and a sense of fulfilment, Jane went to the dining table and began to eat her food. What her elder brothers could not do, little Jane did.

Some stepmothers create problems of rivalry in their homes through their behaviour towards their stepchildren. This attitude of theirs most times leads them into many vices that enable them to achieve their aims through the adoption of a rule system or strategy in the home. These acts of wickedness also lead them into evil practices as well. They do this because they see the stepchild as a competitor to their own children. However, every act of wickedness by stepparents towards their stepchild, or even other people, should be discouraged. People who do evil should also know that there is a payday for their actions here on Earth.

Edwin was angry at the revelation of little Jane, but he did not show his anger in front of the children. So, he waited until the children slept to caution Victoria. He said to her, "Please do not divide or separate my children. James is my first son; you knew about him before I married you. Hillary and the others are his younger siblings. Let this attitude of yours towards James be the last in this house or else."

"Or else what?" Victoria snapped.

"I am warning you for the very last time, do not sow seeds of hatred amongst them."

Edwin in his consternation and disbelief muttered to himself, "I never knew you would be like this. Looking at your humility before me and my people on the days we visited before performing all the marital rights. I remembered you promised to treat and take James as your own child. But today I am seeing a different you. Human beings cannot be predicted and trusted."

Some people can portray themselves as innocent as a lamb before other people or their benefactor, this is a total reflection of ourselves before the mirror. In that reflection, our real self is hidden while we appear innocent outwardly. This was a typical example of James' stepmother. Because most people live a life of falsehood by pretending to be what they are not, it leads them into covering their faults, and hatred for other people. Madam Victoria was guilty of this. Her aim was to shame and turn James into a laughingstock.

From that moment on, Edwin woke up from his slumber and lived up to the expectations to monitor the activities of his wife in the house. It looked like the visit of Anne and the complaints of Jane woke him up to act as the head of his home. James began to enjoy fair treatment and recognition in the house.

The reality is that some of the ill-treatment against stepchildren could be stopped or minimised if the father or mother of the child acted against it. This was the case with James after the incident. The boldness of Jane to reject her food and subsequently report to her father, was a total victory for better treatment of James in that house and by extension, victory for better treatment of other people that would act like little Jane to save the day.

James moved on with his life and resolved to forgive his stepmother and all the mistreatment of him. Life is sweet when we forgive our past and those that caused us pain through one act of wickedness or the other. Forgiveness is one of the secrets of success in life. James grasped it, utilized it and became successful, and this made it possible for him to disabuse the minds and expectations of those that wanted to see him down. It is always easy to come out of such situations as James did if we have a positive mindset in place of a defeatist attitude that leaves some people to self-pity. Victoria too changed her attitude towards James because she listened to the warnings of her husband. Life will continue to be sweet each time we realise our mistakes and correct them because there is no gain in doing evil or wickedness to one another. Stepchildren in our marriages should be taken and treated as our own children too and not abused.

Stepchildren should not allow the activities of stepmothers and stepfathers to lead them into taking their lives. It is disheartening to read stories like that in the daily newspapers. Imagine a situation where you tried and failed to commit suicide, then you end up having a permanent disability that incapacitates you for your lifetime. Invariably you have made the day of the people that pushed you, as you become a burden to them and to yourself, as well as a laughingstock at their mercy. Realising this, suicide should not be an option for anyone to run away from life's challenges.

6

James the Man With a Large Heart

Life at some point gives us an opportunity to give back because there is always a payback period for every good or evil deed against humanity. It is a period in which some people decide to settle scores with those that offended or did them evil by asking for their pound of flesh. But James, the man with a large heart, looked away from any form of revenge. He forgave and brought every member of his father's house together in one love. He preached peace, forgiveness, love and reconciliation in his father's house, to the shame and astonishment of Victoria who had expected mistreatment in return for her attitude towards James. Nature has a way of humbling people,

Madam Victoria, the lioness became bedridden with an unknown illness. She could no longer exert her authority and hatred against James anymore, she had become as meek as a lamb. The world we live in is full of mysteries and it knows how to humble people.

James saw his experience at the hands of his stepmother as part of the training that contributed to making and shaping his life today. Though from all indications, Madam Victoria meant evil by oppressing him, it turned out to be the ladder of his ascension to greatness at the expense of her own children who she valued more than James. Even when the joke was on

James, that he would never succeed or be anything in his father's house. James did everything within his reach to prove his stepmother wrong.

Today, he is the financial pillar of the house. He is also the pathfinder; through him, his stepmother and her children had a say in the community. She had been humbled as she was made to swallow her pride in shame. What a world we live in with its surprises. We should know that the pride of the wicked has no joy at the end of time. She underrated the value of what she would get from James in future, hence she acted and treated him the way she did. This is not peculiar to stepmothers alone but also to other people who have sold their minds to the devil and are determined to do evil.

Madam Victoria felt that she had seen it all, hence her attitude towards James. She also felt that she knew James' future and whatever happened that James would be nobody in life. But she failed to realise that all that glitters is not gold, man proposes but God has the final say. If she had known that God has the final say in James' life, she would have treated him with love.

James did not allow his experience to determine his dealings and relationship with his stepmother, even though he could recall all that he went through in the house. One such was the day his grandparents came and took him to live with them in the village for a while. The fact remained that it did not have a negative impact on James. Neither did it make him follow bad friends to do evil. It did not make him live an anti-social life of stealing, smoking and fighting. But he used the ladder of wickedness against him to climb to his pinnacle of success. He did not become a product of his environment.

Another incident James recalled was when Victoria and Edwin were flexing their muscles in the early hours of the morning over a long-heated argument. The speed of each blow from Edwin can be compared to the speed of each blow thrown by Mohammed Ali and Joe Frazier in their days. Victoria was at the receiving end and to defend herself, she lifted a hard object to hit Edwin. At this point, James tried to separate them, and Victoria angrily said,

"If not for what people would say, James, I would have landed this object on your head, you little brat."

This incident made James vow never to interfere in their matters anymore lest they used him to settle their grievances.

It is good to defeat evil with good. It is also good to be nice to those that did you evil, if only so they will know and understand that with all their evil and wickedness, they cannot change the programme of God in your life. Then they will have a rethink and learn to act with caution. If they also realise that the secrets of their actions and deeds would one day be revealed and that what would be, would be, as determined and decided by God, they would refrain from evil and wickedness.

Victoria's quest to suppress James led her into a shameful and disgraceful situation. Victoria licked her wounds in pain and sorrow. James became the breadwinner and paid all the bills after his father lost his job. Looking back, James realised that it was his experience at the hands of Victoria that changed his world and made him what he was. In life, kindness, love and forgiveness should be in our actions to all, even when people like Victoria fail to know that being kind can be rewarded handsomely. Therefore, stepmothers should care for and treat other people's children the same way they would want their own children to be treated. Mistreating your stepchild or even your house help because you feel or believe no one can protect him or her from you is unacceptable.

James the man of the moment with a large heart knew that in every ill-treatment and wickedness, there was always something good to dig out of it. He realised the value of hard work and the value of the human being from all that he went through, then assured himself that he would be successful. He put behind him all the acts of Victoria which were intended to frustrate him. But in the face of all these, he was determined to succeed. This attitude of James is expected of everyone that is going through one difficult situation at home or elsewhere.

Undeniably, most people who have gone through ill-treatment in life have been known to come out strong and successful because they maintained a positive approach during and after the period. James aimed high to succeed amid his travails because he saw light at the end of the tunnel.

James worked with every piece of advice he got from his father. He remembered the day his father said to him, "James, my son, if you allow the seed of what you passed through in the hands of your stepmother, to grow into an iroko tree in your heart, you would end up living a life of revenge and this will defeat the plan and purpose of God for your life. Therefore, be ready to forgive your stepmother for everything she did to you." These words resonated several times in his subconscious.

Following his father's advice, James did not wait for apologies from his stepmother to forgive her for all the wrongs she did to him. Though she denied doing any harm to James, even when it was disclosed that she visited a fetish priest to destabilise and frustrate James. Of course, evil doers most times find it difficult to own up or accept their evil deeds when confronted with them because of the shame it would bring afterwards. But her position in all of these was immaterial to James who had decided to move on with his life. Who would even believe that his stepmother could be diabolical in her actions to silence him? This was one of the reasons James considered his father's advice.

From that moment on, James vowed to forgive everyone that did one thing or the other to hurt him in the past, without waiting for their apologies. People should know that life is complementary, and we live to build each other up because of tomorrow. Though he was aggrieved that someone he trusted, called mother at some point could be so malicious and wicked as to treat him like trash in his father's house. He forgave her, loved and cared for her thus dismantling the mountain of revenge in his heart before now.

A case where some people take advantage of our rights and privileges to do us evil because they are in a position of authority is not different from some stepmothers who take children's bread to give it to the dogs. James showed love to all when he built a magnificent edifice to house his father's household. He believed in the principle of forgiveness, and he asked God to forgive his stepmother too because he believed she did not know what she did.

James realised he was in an environment of opportunities. He never wanted sympathy or pity for what he went through to define him, nor did he allow his environment to shape his life. Hence, he brushed aside his experience to soar like the eagle. Stepchildren should not limit themselves by recoiling to self-pity.

James learnt to develop thick skin towards his challenges. He did not allow the situation in his father's house to take the better part of him, so he did not sink into the mire of his troubles. Remarkably, aeroplanes do not crash because of the air surrounding them, but they crash when air enters them. James realised he was the aeroplane in his father's house and all the troubles he went through were the hot air from his stepmother. Stepchildren should strive to be the eagles that soar above all the other birds, even during storms. BRAVO to all stepchildren and house helps and others who may be going through mistreatment at the hands of those that promised to protect YOU.

7

The Power of Forgiveness

Forgiveness is important if we want to move on in life to fulfil our aims and goals. A life of unforgiveness leads to disaster. Forgiveness helps us to remove any string that would hold us back from moving forward. Inwardly, you are clean, pure and free to move on. James realised this when he decided to forgive his stepmother. According to him, her ill-treatment was a stepping stone to what contributed to making him a real man. Everyone aspires to be real and successful in life to strike dumb those that wanted to see them down.

We show maturity when we overlook our past travails and disappointments at the hands of people who treated us badly. We show love to them because there is no gain in revenge or paying back to our past offenders. James is a good example to emulate. His mother's advice to him played a role in his decision to forgive all. He remembered the words of his mother, "My son, never pay back evil with evil, rather do good to those that offended you. The life we live today is not our own, it belongs to God, and He will hold us accountable for our acts." This was good advice from a good, loving and God-fearing mother. I wish all mothers would be like her.

James believed in his father's family and his father's words to him too. According to his father, "Family is a place where existence begins and love for one another should never cease or be compromised on the altar of hatred, irrespective of our shortcomings." Yes, togetherness in the family makes us a formidable front, so stepmothers should stop this attitude of hatred and divide-and-rule mentality against the stepchild. God chooses our family for us; He brought you into that family to help and build it, not to divide it or tear it apart. He blessed you in that home with a stepchild to care for and nurture for a purpose. To this effect, stepmothers should endeavour to be a symbol of strength and stability in homes to build and promote unity and progress, where no one is discriminated against.

When James remembered his past, and saw his stepmother the tyrant, becoming as meek as a lamb, and the tigress tamed in her present condition, he asked, "What is in this world that makes us do evil and wickedness to people under our care?" Of course, age had played a fast one on both Edwin and Victoria as they were advanced in age. If people will remember this stage in their existence and behave well to other people, realising they would one day take responsibility for their actions, this world would be a better place for all.

James saw his father's family as his greatest treasure, and he decided to forgive them and brought them all under one roof because family is a unit of co-existence and the bond that links us together should be unbroken, no matter what. This is victory over wickedness. Madam Victoria observed that her pride had taken a beating from the way James treated her and others. What she expected for ill-treating James was not what she got in return. However, the success of James in the face of all hostilities was a victory, not only for him but for all stepchildren and other people who go through hard times and abuse at the hands of stepmothers and the like.

One good day, Edwin invited James to his room to have a father-and-son discussion when everybody had gone out. Victoria had gone to the hospital for routine treatment. Edwin said to James, "My son, always be proud of yourself when you are at your best, act with integrity and do the right thing at the right time. I was very proud of you when I learnt of the decisions you made concerning the family. Always be yourself and the person that will look others in the face and tell them the truth, no matter how painful and difficult it will look at the time. Do not be the praise singer man to deceive the people but be the man that will stand your ground, to tell the truth always.

"Secondly, I wanted you to note that I threw away my diamond on the altar of fear by trying to obey and please my parents. I lost a woman of virtue who would have used her light to paint and brighten my darkness. She was no other woman than Anne, your mother. Forgive my foolishness and learn from my mistakes. Learn to always follow your mind to succeed in this hostile world where people we trust betray us as a result of envy."

After a long silence, James thanked him and promised to do as he advised and got up to leave when he said to him, "Wait, I have not finished, my son. Do not allow sentiments to overrule your sense of judgment on matters brought to you, even when someone close to you is involved in the matter. Just know that I am very proud of you because you are not a product of your environment where envy, hatred and wickedness reigned supreme."

James was thankful to his father and got up to attend to other things. But he did not realise that these were the parting words from his father before he gave up the ghost some days later.

After his death and a befitting burial, James gathered his father's house together to determine what the future would look like. This act by him was meant to douse the fear of the reality that settled on his stepmother's mind that James would maltreat her. She was fearful of the shadow of her acts against him the moment she received the call that made her a widow. She remembered her ill-treatment against James and became afraid as it dawned on her that her past had caught up with her.

But James was a man of peace who never wanted to pay back with evil. He was the first person to console her with words of assurance to look after her. He was conscious of his next move in life as he began to live his life to mitigate his father's experiences and mistakes.

His father lived the life of other people by doing things to please them. He did not identify who he was and wanted to be early in life. This is dangerous as it leads to comparing someone's success with yours and this inevitably breeds jealousy.

This was the case with Gilbert and Jonah. And James had learnt a whole lot from that. Always be yourself to live your dreams. It may hurt but you will come out happy. When you overcome fear, in the middle of your difficulties and decisions you will soar and ascend to accomplish your goals. Let it be known that James achieved success and victory because he put in everything, he had gained from his experience into everything he did to succeed.

Experience remains our best teacher in life, so the emptiness and the fear of failure created in James by the acts of his stepmother towards him in his growing up days raised the desire and hunger in him to succeed in life beyond her expectations. The more some stepmothers learn to remove emotions and passion from their hatred towards the stepchild and create a level playground of love and recognition of the stepchild in their homes, the better, sweeter, happier and more peaceful the home becomes. This will only be possible when they stop seeing the stepchild as an error of creation or as a visitor or even as a threat to their own children, but rather let them see the stepchild as God's masterpiece in His creative work who did not find himself or herself in that family by accident.

Then stepchildren in any home should see themselves as champions in the family and should not allow themselves to be intimidated by anyone in the family. The time has come when the narrative and attitude of some stepmothers to kill their stepchild before they grow up must stop. And parents should desist from breaking relationships of their children for whatever reason, except where life is threatened as this may help to check the emergence of a stepmother in the home.

James put his past behind him and vowed never to hold it against his stepmother. He remembered the parting words of his father and promised to show love and care to her and his half-brothers and sister. This is true love from a heart that forgives because forgiving your offenders, both in the past and present will help you to move on with your life. This was James' position and he succeeded at last. Be like James by knowing and realising the fact that you can achieve your potential in life when you know and believe that your history or background is not your destiny and cannot define, determine or decide your destiny.

The success story of James became the evening news on the lips of everyone in the neighbourhood because he did not allow the attitude of his stepmother towards him to determine or shape his life. Some people would have used ill-treatment to excuse revenge or even given up on life.

Available worldwide from Amazon

Michael Terence Publishing

www.mtp.agency

mtp.agency

@mtp_agency

Printed in Dunstable, United Kingdom

71980949R00047